First day at School

PaRragon

Bath · New York · Singapore · Hong Kong · Cologne · Delhi
Melbourne · Amsterdam · Johannesburg · Auckland · Shenzhen

How to Use This Book

 Read the story, all about Mia, Luke, and Sophie, and their first day at school.

 Look closely at each picture in the story. You may be asked to find or count things in a scene and place a sticker on the page.

 Try each activity as you go along, or read the story first, then go back and do the activities. The answers are at the bottom of each activity page.

 Some pictures will need stickers to finish the scenes or activities. Any leftover stickers can be used to decorate the book or your things.

Mia, Luke, and Sophie are ready
for their first day at school.

Find these things outside the school.

They have their bags and lunch boxes,
and each one has brought a special friend!

Now put a lunch box
sticker here.

Match each child to his or her teddy bear, and then match the teddy bear to the child's bag.

Answer

When they get to school, Ms. Rose and her helper, Annie, are there to welcome them.

Annie helps the children find hooks for their coats and cubbies for their bags and lunch boxes.

Find the stickers to finish the picture.

Find these things in the classroom.

Mia's cubby has a rainbow. Sophie's cubby has a sun. Luke's cubby has a lion.

Count the name labels.

Sam

Sophie

Luke

Mia

Ava

Find the rocket sticker.

Annie shows the three friends their table.
A little boy is already there. His name is Jake,
and he is drawing a picture of a car.

"I like cars," says Jake. "They're my favorite thing to draw."

Can you help
Sophie and Luke
count things
in the classroom?

How many red
tables?

How many
blue chairs?

How many
yellow boxes?

What other
colors can
you see?

Find the stickers to finish the picture.

Ms. Rose and Annie help the children choose what to do. Mia decides to play at the sand box.

Can you find these things in the classroom?

Sophie likes the water play.
And Luke wants to paint a picture.

Now find the boat sticker.

It's lunchtime! Mia, Sophie, and Luke are eating sandwiches and fruit. "What do you have for lunch, Jake?" asks Sophie.

Can you find these things in the picture?

Answer

Lunchtime is over, and the children
rush outside to play.

Find these things in the playground.

Sophie likes to climb. Luke goes through the tunnel. Mia plays on the seesaw with Jake.

What color is the big toy car?

Now find the duck sticker.

When they are back inside, the children sit quietly while Ms. Rose reads them a story. Their cuddly friends listen to the story too!

Can you find five differences between these two pictures?

Answer

After story time, Annie sings a song
with the children.

The wheels on the bus
go round and round,
round and round,
round and round.
The wheels on the bus
go round and round,
all through the town.

It's "The Wheels on the Bus."
"That's my favorite song!" says Jake.

The wheels on the bus
go round and round,
round and round,
round and round.
The wheels on the bus
go round and round,
all through the town.

Sing along
to this song!

Help clean up the classroom. Point to where each thing belongs.

dollhouse

pail

book

shelves

doll

sand box

blocks

box

Answer

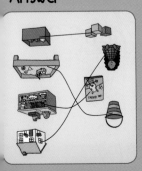

Time to go home! The children go to their hooks and cubbies to get their things. Uh-oh! Luke can't find his teddy bear! The others help him look.

Help the children find these things too!

"He's on the green mat!" says Mia.
"I think Luke's teddy bear wants
to stay at school!" says Sophie.

"Don't worry," Luke tells his teddy bear. "We can come back to school tomorrow. I can't wait!"